This igloo book belongs to:

....

igloobooks

Published in 2012
by Igloo Books Ltd
Cottage Farm
Sywell
NN6 0BJ
www.igloobooks.com

FIR003 1112
4 6 8 10 9 7 5 3
ISBN: 978-0-85780-429-7

Printed and manufactured in China

Trunk Trouble

igloobooks

Little Elephant loves playing with his friends.
They run and jump and laugh together.
But today they can't think of any games to play.
Today they are just too hot.

"What shall we do?" asks Little Elephant.
"Play in the cool, shady spots," says his mother.

First, the friends play hide-and-seek.
Little Lion Cub counts to ten.

"One . . .

. . .two . . .

. . .three . .

Crocodile hides in the water.

Little Monkey hides in a leafy tree.
Little Tiger hides in the long, yellow grass.

But Little Elephant is too big.
He can't find anywhere to hide!

..."ten!" roars Little Lion Cub. "Coming, ready or not!"
"There's nowhere for me to go!" cries Little Elephant.

He tries to hide behind a bush.
But his long trunk sticks out!

THUMP! BUMP! BANG!

Little Lion Cub trips over Little Elephant's trunk!

"Ouch!" cries Little Lion Cub. "You and your big nose!"

Little Elephant blushes bright red. "I'm sorry," he whispers.

"I don't want to play anymore," sniffs Little Lion Cub.

Poor Little Elephant feels sad.
He didn't mean to spoil the game.

The friends try playing ball.
At first, they have lots of fun.

They run up and down, round and round.
Little Armadillo rolls around and does cartwheels.

But all that running around
makes clouds of dust . . .

. . . and the dust gets
up Little Elephant's nose. . .

AHHHHCHOOOOO!

Little Elephant's sneeze blows Little Armadillo into the bushes!

"You and your big nose!"
cries Little Armadillo.

Little Elephant hangs his head down.
"I think I'll go for a walk," he mumbles.
And he trudges away by himself.

Poor Little Elephant starts to cry.

"Don't worry," says his mother, as she gives him a cuddle.

"Why are you crying, Little Elephant?" she asks.
"My trunk is too long!" he wails.
"It gets in the way of our games."
"I know something you can play,"
says Little Elephant's mother.
"Let's go and find your friends."
And she whispers her plan in his ear.

Little Elephant's friends are splashing in
the waterhole.

"The waterhole is boring" says Little Tiger.
Little Elephant smiles.

He fills his trunk with water.
"Maybe I can help!" says
Little Elephant.

SPLOOSH!
SPLASH!

Little Elephant trumpets water high into the air and all over his friends.

"Fantastic!" laughs Little Lion Cub.

"Thanks, everyone!" says Little Elephant. "Now I'm happy . . .

. . . Just as I am."